Grandmama's Pride

Becky Birtha

Illustrated by Colin Bootman

Albert Whitman & Company
Morton Grove, Illinois

For my mother and father, Jessie Moore Birtha and Herbert Marshall Birtha,
and remembering my grandmother, Feddie Adele Dixon Moore.—B.B.

To all grandmothers.—C.B.

Library of Congress Cataloging-in-Publication Data

Birtha, Becky, 1948-
Grandmama's pride / by Becky Birtha ; illustrated by Colin Bootman.
p. cm.
Summary: While on a trip in 1956 to visit her grandmother in the South, six-year-old Sarah Marie experiences segregation for the first time,
but discovers that things have changed by the time she returns the following year.
ISBN 10: 0-8075-3028-X (hardcover) ISBN 13: 978-0-8075-3028-3 (hardcover)
[1. Segregation—Fiction. 2. Grandmothers—Fiction. 3. Civil rights movements—United States—History—20th century. 4. African Americans—Fiction.
5. Southern States—History—1951—Fiction. 6. United States—History—1953-1961—Fiction.] I. Bootman, Colin, ill. II. Title.
PZ7.B52337Gra 2005 [Fic]—dc22 2005003991

The art is rendered in watercolor on paper.
The design is by Colin Bootman and Carol Gildar.

For more information about Albert Whitman & Company,
please visit our web site at www.albertwhitman.com.

Our family lived up north, but every summer when school was out, Mama, Sister, and I went down south to stay at Grandmama's house. The summer of 1956, Sister was five and I was six.

"The back seat is the best seat on the bus," Mama explained while we waited inside the bus station. "It's big and wide and roomy, and the two of you won't bother anybody. Plus, it's right next to the bathroom."

Our bus pulled in! Mama waited for our bags to be loaded while Sister and I climbed aboard to find a seat. "Go all the way back, Sarah Marie," Mama reminded me. Sister and I didn't know there was a law that said only white people could ride down south in the front of the bus.

We rode all morning. By lunchtime Mama told us we had reached Maryland. "We're in the South now," she said.

The bus pulled into a rest stop, and we got off to stretch our legs. A lot of people headed for the lunch counter, and I did, too. But Mama caught me up quick.

"We brought our own lunches, Sarah Marie, remember?" she said.

Back on the bus, Mama unpacked our sandwiches, potato chips in silver foil bags, and a peach apiece.

After lunch Mama read us stories. Soon I'd be able to read, too. Aunt Maria, Mama's sister who lived near Grandmama, was going to teach me how, just like she taught all the first grade kids in her class.

Sister and I played "I Spy" and counted cows and horses. We fell asleep and woke up and rode some more. Finally, we were there!

COLORED
WAITING ROOM

WHI
WAIT

The bus station in Grandmama's town had two
waiting rooms, but only one had benches for sitting down.
Grandmama and Aunt Maria were in the stand-up waiting
room. Grandmama's next-door neighbor, Reverend Daniels,
was there, too. He took us to her house in his shiny black
Plymouth.

As soon as we arrived, Grandmama started cooking. After that there was always something good to eat. Dinner was fried chicken and potato salad, stewed tomatoes, buttery rolls, and greens. Grandmama cooked every kind of greens you could think of— mustard, turnip, creesie, and dandelion greens, poke salad, collards, and kale.

Dessert was a big juicy golden peach pie.

Next morning, nobody was in a hurry. The stretched-out, down-south, summertime days were here. Sister and I swung in the garden and chalked hopscotches up and down the sidewalk. We played paper dolls on the screened-in upstairs porch, and cut out their dresses from last year's Sears Roebuck catalog. We colored pictures to mail to Daddy, and waited a week for a letter back. We didn't call anybody. Grandmama had no telephone.

One morning Grandmama told us to put on shoes, not sandals, and wash our hands and faces. We were going downtown to buy material for new dresses.

"Are we going to catch the bus?" Sister asked. She was too little to remember Grandmama's peculiar ways. But I remembered from last summer. Grandmama never rode the bus.

"God gave us each two good strong legs for walking," Grandmama told Sister. She fastened her hat on with a ruby hatpin, held her black umbrella high to shade her from the sun, and stepped out proud in her black lace-up shoes. Sister and I came stepping right behind her. And we walked.

We didn't know that Grandmama refused to take the downtown bus, where people our color had to ride in the rear. We didn't know that Grandmama's pride was too tall to fit in the back of a bus.

At the dry goods store, Grandmama chose gingham and seersucker for our summer dresses. Then we walked to the post office.

Outside the post office, by a big sign, we spotted a gleaming water fountain.

Sister and I were thirsty, but Grandmama told us, "I don't want you drinking from a public water fountain. You don't know who's been drinking there. Wait until we get home. Grandmama's going to fix you ice-cold, lemon-mint tea from fresh-squeezed lemons, with spearmint out of my garden."

Sister and I walked right by that water fountain. We knew Grandmama's iced tea was better than any water anywhere.

WHITE ONLY

The next day the sewing began. All day long we heard the slippery rocking rhythm of the foot treadle on Grandmama's sewing machine.

While Grandmama and Mama sewed, Aunt Maria was teaching me how to read. By July I could read words all over the kitchen.

The next time we walked the ten blocks downtown, in the hot August sun, I could read the names of all the streets we passed. At the hardware store, we bought some twine, onion sets for fall planting, and a new broom. I read the names on all the bags of seeds.

COLORED
WOMEN

WHITE
WOMEN

Then Sister needed to use the bathroom. Grandmama told
Mama, "Take her into the bus station. It's right around the corner."

We hurried through the sit-down waiting room and down a
hall. Sister ran over to a door with a picture of a lady's head. I read
the sign at the top of the door. It said, "White Women."

Mama pulled Sister back in a hurry. "Not this bathroom,"
she said, and took us to a different one, farther down the hall.

"Colored Women," this sign said. There wasn't any toilet
paper or soap.

When we came out, I started to look around me. The signs had been there all along, but now I could read them. Four different bathrooms!

WHITE ONLY

WHITE MEN

COLORED MEN

There was a water fountain in the bus station, too. The sign over it didn't say "Water." It said "White Only."

I asked Grandmama why those signs were there.

"Sarah Marie, I'm very proud of you for learning how to read," she said. "But I'm sorry you have to read these hateful signs. This is the South, and we still have segregation down here. That means we have separate places for colored folks and white folks. Some grown folks still don't seem to understand that we're, all of us, God's children."

She looked at the White Only water fountain, and leaned down to me. "But you don't want that city water anyway," she said. "It isn't even cold."

Our last stop was the five and ten. At the lunch counter, hot dogs sizzled on the grill. A sign hung over the lunch counter, too.

It seemed like a long, long walk back home.

The next time Grandmama and Mama and Sister went downtown, I asked to stay home with Aunt Maria. She wanted to listen to me read. But I didn't feel like reading anything. I was ready for the summer to be over, ready to go home, far away from unfair signs and laws.

On the day we left, Grandmama made us sandwiches. She packed a tin of homemade cookies and a peach apiece. Aunt Maria took our pictures beside the crepe myrtle tree out front.

We loaded our suitcases into the trunk of Reverend Daniels's shiny black Plymouth, and rode back to the bus station.

We went to the stand-up waiting room and watched out the window for our bus. Sister wanted to go in the other waiting room and sit down.

Mama and Grandmama looked at each other. Through the glass door between the two rooms, I could see the sign that Sister couldn't read yet. I put my arm around Sister's shoulders. "You don't want to sit on those public benches," I told her. "You don't know who's been sitting there."

Grandmama gave me a surprised look, then smiled. "Why, Sarah Marie!" she said. "You took the words right out of my mouth."

WHI
WAITIN

BUS BOYCOTT ENDS IN VICTORY

When we said goodbye, Aunt Maria left red lipstick
kisses on our cheeks. I told Grandmama I'd be back next
summer, but I wasn't sure I wanted to.

Back home, up north, there weren't any segregation signs.
I wasn't afraid of what words might say, and I read everything.

That fall Mama and Daddy's newspapers told about
faraway places, like Clinton, Tennessee, where kids like Sister
and me intended to go to better schools, no matter what.
There were pictures of Montgomery, Alabama, where no
colored people would ride on the buses, even in the winter.
Until they could sit where they wanted, everybody walked,
just like Grandmama.

I read words I didn't understand. Boycott. Ballot.
Civil Rights. Supreme Court Ruling. Laws Overturned.

When summer came and it was time to go down south again, Mama got on the bus first. "Let's try something different this time," she said. And we rode all the way down south in the front seat of that bus.

At the rest stop, Mama told us we could get off the bus, sit down at the lunch counter, and have a drink. I had an orange soda, and Sister had grape.

When our bus arrived, Grandmama wasn't waiting on the platform or in the stand-up waiting room. She was in the sit-down waiting room.

Sister had to use the bathroom. I did, too. Grandmama said she'd take us. Then my grandmama walked, with her tall, proud steps, across the floor of that white waiting room, and straight to the door of the white women's bathroom.

I hung back. I didn't know what would happen.

"I thought you needed to use the restroom, Sarah Marie," Grandmama said.

"I did," I mumbled. "But isn't this the wrong one?"

Grandmama looked up at the door and I did, too. The sign there just said "Women."

"You can forget about the other signs," Grandmama said. "We held our ground and got those laws struck down." She laughed. "Those days are gone forever!"

WOMEN

Grandmama raised her arm, pushed open the door, and strode right in. And Sister and I were stepping right behind her.

Author's Note

Grandmama's Pride is a fictional story based on real events and memories of the 1950s, when segregation kept black and white Americans apart in the southern United States. Laws and customs there did not allow African Americans many of the rights and freedoms that everyone in the North enjoyed.

African Americans, known then as Negroes or colored people, could not use the same drinking fountains and bathrooms as whites. Waiting rooms and movie theaters had separate seating areas. Many public libraries did not allow African Americans at all.

On buses, whether going across town or to another state, black riders had to give seats in the front to white passengers. Traveling from the North to the South, they might have to get up and change seats before the bus crossed the Mason-Dixon line—the dividing line between northern and southern states.

Lunch counters and restaurants served either white or black customers, but not both, so many black travelers carried their own meals. Sarah Marie's grandmother enjoyed sewing, but also knew that the family would not be allowed to try on clothing in stores.

In the newspapers in late 1956, Sarah Marie read about the success of the Montgomery, Alabama, bus boycott. When Rosa Parks was arrested there because she would not give up her seat on the bus to a white rider, the Rev. Dr. Martin Luther King, Jr., led black citizens in refusing to ride the racially segregated city buses. After more than a year, they won the right to sit where they chose. Sarah Marie read about brave children who took great risks for equal education. Although the United States Supreme Court had outlawed segregation in public schools in May 1954, in many schools the first black students to enter still faced threats and hostility.

Grandmama's town chose to end segregation in the bus terminal in 1957, soon after it was outlawed on city buses nationwide by a Supreme Court ruling. But in most cities and counties of the Deep South, such changes did not come until 1961, when groups of white and black Freedom Riders rode buses together throughout the southern United States to bring national attention to the unequal segregated waiting rooms, restrooms, and restaurants.

A few years later, Congress passed the Civil Rights Act of 1964, outlawing discrimination based on race, color, religion, or national origin in restaurants, hotels, theaters, and other public places, as well as in employment and voting.

Sarah Marie's experience is just one story in the Civil Rights Movement, the struggle for people of all races to be treated equally.

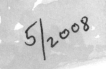

5/2008